P9-CLY-030

# The Mouses' Terrible Christmas

True Kelley &
Steven Lindblom

Lothrop, Lee & Shepard Company
A Division of William Morrow & Company, Inc.
New York

Library of Congress Cataloging in Publication Data
Kelley, True.
The Mouses' terrible Christmas.
(A fun-to-read book)
SUMMARY: It's Christmas at the Mouses' where holiday havoc is a family tradition.
[1. Christmas stories. 2. Mice—Fiction. 3. Humorous stories] I. Lindblom, Steven, joint author. II. Title.
PZ7.K2824Mo [Fic] 78-6995
ISBN 0-688-41856-2
ISBN 0-688-51856-7 lib. bdg.



Printed in the United States of America.
First Edition
1 2 3 4 5 6 7 8 9 10

CONTENTS

# THE PERFECT TREE

The Mouse family was getting ready for Christmas. Their farmhouse was clean and sparkling, the mistletoe was hung, the wreath was on the front door.

Mums and Dad Mouse and the children, Emily and Fred, went out to look for a Christmas tree.

"Look!" cried Fred. "The perfect tree!"

They all agreed it was the nicest tree they had ever seen. Mums raised the axe to make the first chop.

"NO NO NO!" cried the other Mouses. "It's much too nice a tree to chop down!"

"You're right," said Mums, putting the axe down. "I couldn't bear to kill it."

They were all sad for a moment at the thought.

The Mouses trudged on until they came to another tree. It wasn't nearly as nice as the first one.

"Well, no one will miss *this* tree," said Dad. "But if we put the bad side to the wall, it will look fine."

Mums raised the axe again.

"Oh, don't!" cried Emily. "It's such a poor little tree. It must have had a terrible life, but it's made it this far. It wouldn't be fair to chop it down, now!"

The thought made them all sad again.

They walked on in silence.
"Why, here's a tree!" Mums cried out. "And it's already cut for us!"
"That's just the Groundchucks' old tree from last year," groaned Fred and Emily.
"Nonsense," Dad said. "It's a wonderful tree. And it already has tinsel on it!"

"It looks pretty dried out," said Fred, doubtfully.
"Only one side has needles left," said Emily.
"We'll put the bare side to the wall," said Dad.
"It's very practical," said Mums. "I bet it will look nice next year, too."
So they carefully carried it home.

## A TERRIBLE CRASH

That evening after supper, the Mouses trimmed their tree. It was slow, careful work to hang the ornaments without knocking off the needles.

STAR

“Here,” Mums said, “I’ve made some popcorn to string and hang on the tree.”

The Mouses set to work on it.

It was late when they finished.

That night was the night before the night before Christmas. Emily and Fred dreamed about Santa.

Outside, the wind began to howl.

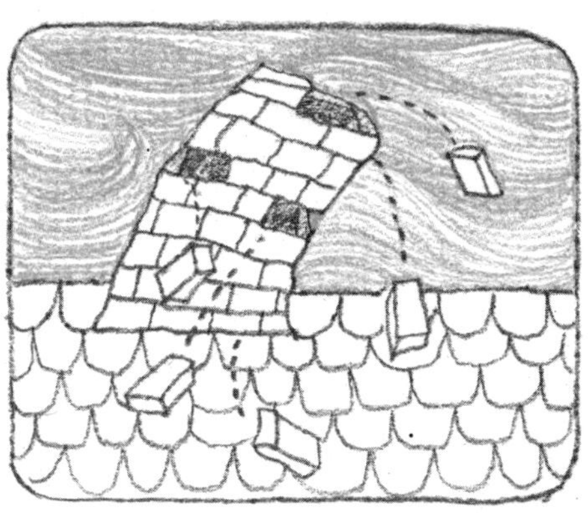

Suddenly there was a
terrible CRASH.
The chimney had blown down into
a million broken bricks!

"Oh, no!" said Mums.

"Oh, NO!" said Emily and Fred. "How will Santa get in? We'll never get it fixed by Christmas!" They both started to cry.

"Don't worry, we'll rig up something in the morning," mumbled Dad.

He and Mums went back to sleep.

Fred and Emily worried all night.

At dawn, they woke up Mums and Dad.
"It's the day before Christmas!" they cried. "We've got to build a chimney for Santa, quick!"

Dad got out a pile of old cardboard, a hammer and nails, and some red paint.

The Mouses carried everything up to the roof.

Mums painted bricks on the cardboard, and Dad shaped it into a chimney and nailed it down.

Emily and Fred were very happy with it.

When the Mouses got back inside they were cold from being up on the roof, so Mums made a big pot of tea.

Dad lit a nice warm fire in the fireplace.

"I smell cardboard burning,"
said Emily.

"Oh, NO! The CHIMNEY!"
cried Fred.

They all clambered up onto the roof with the pot of tea.

Mums threw tea on the flaming cardboard chimney.

But there wasn't enough tea to put out the fire.

Dad ran down to make another pot.

Six pots of tea later the fire was out.
The chimney was a pile of ashes.
There was a big hole burned in the roof.
Snow fell through the hole and into the living room.

Everyone was very depressed.

"Well, let's patch the hole and make another chimney," Mums said at last. "But we'll have to work fast, because Santa will be here soon."

Fred and Mums hastily made another cardboard chimney.

Emily gathered some twigs and branches, and Dad patched the hole in the roof with them.
It was almost dark when they had finished.
They all stood back to admire their work.

"I don't know about that chimney," said Fred. "It looks more like a spotted toadstool."

"I'll make a sign," Emily said, "so Santa will know."

Her sign said:

# THE NIGHT BEFORE CHRISTMAS

After their hard day of chimney building, the Mouses were tired but happy.
It was the night before Christmas, and Santa would be able to come after all.
Mums went to the kitchen to boil up some of her famous Sticky Christmas Candy.

Fred and Emily hung their
Christmas stockings.
Then they guarded the fireplace
to make sure no one tried to
light a fire.
Dad frantically wrapped presents.

"What is that racket outside?" yelled Mums from the kitchen. "Do try and stop it. The carolers will be here any minute."

"But it IS the carolers!" cried Emily and Fred.

They ran to the door and let the carolers in.

← chimney here

Everyone gathered in the living room to sing Christmas carols. Their voices rang out and rose to the patched ceiling.

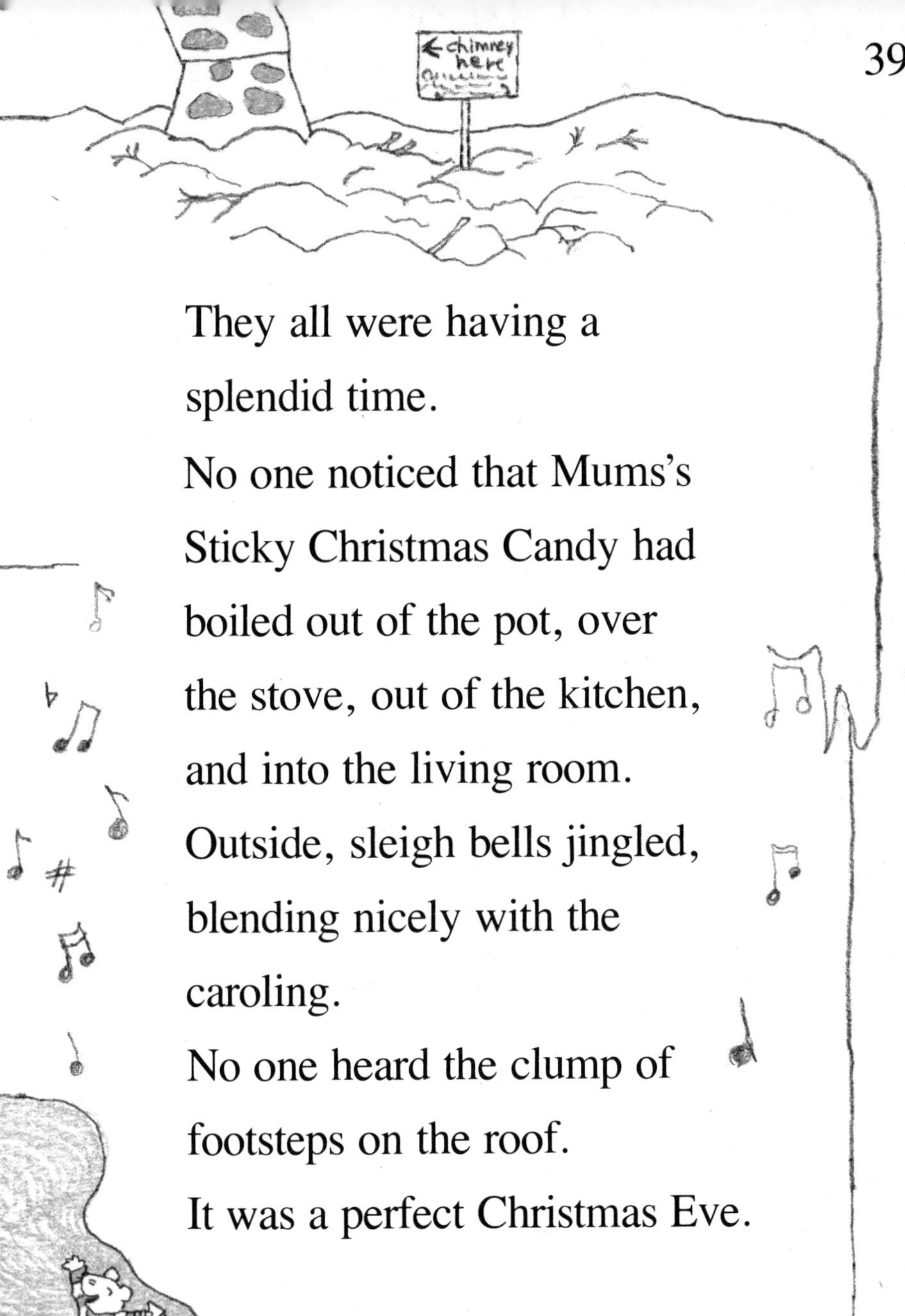


They all were having a splendid time.
No one noticed that Mums's Sticky Christmas Candy had boiled out of the pot, over the stove, out of the kitchen, and into the living room.
Outside, sleigh bells jingled, blending nicely with the caroling.
No one heard the clump of footsteps on the roof.
It was a perfect Christmas Eve.

They had just begun to sing
"Silent Night" when there was
a thump, a thud, and the sound
of breaking branches.
Santa came crashing through
the ceiling in a shower of sticks,
twigs, and snow.

NIGHT

Santa knocked over the carolers, landed in the Sticky Christmas Candy, and bounced into the Christmas tree.

All the dried pine needles that were still on the tree fell off and stuck to the Sticky Christmas Candy that was now stuck to Santa. He looked like a porcupine.

Christmas at the Mouses'

The carolers were NOT caroling.
It was so quiet they could hear
a faint clunk as the wreath
fell off the front door.

Santa started to laugh.

"HO HO HO," he said. "Another Christmas at the Mouses'!"

"That's right," said Dad, "I had forgotten. Almost the same thing happened last year!"

"It all seemed rather familiar to me," said Mums.

"We will NOT be caroling here next year," said the carolers, as they hurried out.
Santa stood up, found his sack, and filled the Mouses' stockings with sticky presents.

“I wouldn’t miss Christmas at the Mouses’ for anything,” he said. “But next year, if you don’t mind, I’ll use the front door.”

## A WHITE CHRISTMAS

When Santa had gone, the Mouses
looked around at their house.
It was a mess!
Dad stood the tree back up,
and Mums rehung the ornaments.
Fred and Emily pulled sticky
pine needles off the floor
and stuck them back on the tree.
Soon the house was almost in
order.

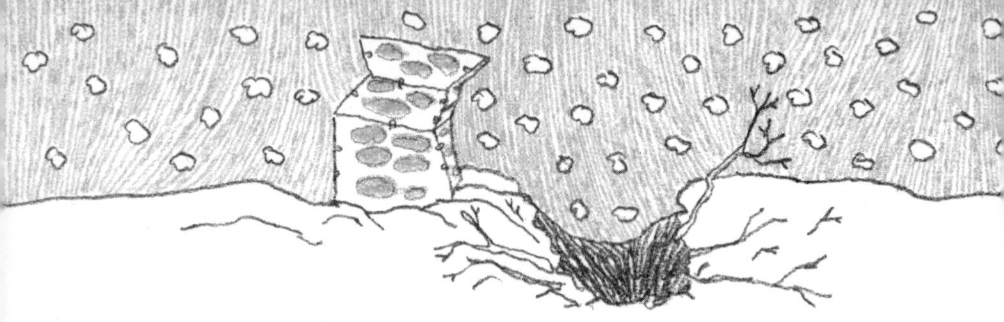

"Well, I guess it's time to go up and patch the hole in the roof again," Dad sighed.

"But the snow looks so lovely falling on the tree," said Mums.

"And the tree needs all the help it can get," added Fred.

"All right, we'll leave it until after Christmas," Dad agreed.

Emily made them all some hot cider with cinnamon sticks.

The Mouses sat together admiring their tree until bedtime.

Late that night, when everyone was asleep, the snow began to fall harder.

The next morning was Christmas! Emily and Fred were in such a hurry to open their stockings that they tumbled down the stairs—right into a giant snowdrift.

"Boy," said Emily, "there must have been a blizzard last night!"

Only the star on top of the Christmas tree poked out of the drift.

"Race you to the stockings!"
yelled Fred.
They burrowed frantically through
the snow towards the fireplace.

The new mittens in their stockings
went right on their cold feet.

When Mums and Dad came down, they found a snowball battle raging. "Oh, NO," groaned Dad. "Stop playing! Get the shovel! Get the brooms! Grandpaw and Grandmaw will be here any minute!"

"The snow does look pretty, though," said Mums.

They shoveled and swept and
swept and shoveled.
Fred rolled huge snowballs out
the front door.
He almost rolled the last one
right into Grandpaw and Grandmaw.

“Oh, dear,” said Grandmaw, as she looked around at the living room. “Well, I guess it’s not as bad as last year.”

“Did Santa make it here last night?” asked Grandpaw.

“He sure did!” replied the Mouses.

“We waited up for him,” Grandmaw said, “but a porcupine came instead!”

“That wasn’t a porcupine—” Fred began.

“Let’s open the presents,” said Dad.

Everyone gathered around the tree.

"Neat-o!" squealed Emily. "A mechanical fish!"

"An inflatable cat!" yelled Fred. "Just what I wanted!"

"Matching butterfly nets!" said Grandmaw and Grandpaw, obviously pleased.

Dad and Mums opened their present from Grandmaw and Grandpaw. It was a new teapot. "We can always use another teapot," Mums said. "Thank you!"

It was a terribly nice Christmas.

TRUE KELLEY and STEVEN LINDBLOM have lived and traveled widely in Europe and Asia, but are now settled in rural New Hampshire, where they divide their time between freelance illustration and country pastimes such as cooking, gardening, beermaking, skiing, and watching the small creatures, mice among them, that are their neighbors and tenants. Collectors of children's books, they have long felt there was a need for a Christmas story that was neither goody-goody nor dull, and *The Mouses' Terrible Christmas* is the lively result.